First United States edition 1992

Margaret K. McElderry Books, Macmillan Publishing Company, 866 Third Avenue, New York, NY 10022

Maxwell Macmillan Canada, Inc., 1200 Eglinton Avenue East, Suite 200, Don Mills, Ontario M3C 3N1

Macmillan Publishing Company is part of the Maxwell Communication Group of Companies.

An international coproduction arranged by Gyldendal, Copenhagen 1991
Illustrations copyright © 1991 by Svend Otto S.
English translation from the Norwegian, copyright © 1992 by Margaret K. McElderry Books, Macmillan Publishing Company

Printed in Denmark   10 9 8 7 6 5 4 3 2 1

Library of Congress Cataloging-in-Publication Data
Asbjørnsen, Peter Christen, 1812–1885.
The man who kept house / by Abjørnsen and Moe ; illustrated by Svend Otto S. — 1st U.S. ed.   p.   cm.
Summary: Convinced that his work in the field is harder than his wife's work at home, a farmer trades places with her for the day.
ISBN 0-689-50560-4 [1. Folklore—Norway.]   I. Moe, Jørgen Engebretsen, 1813–1882. II. Svend Otto S. (Svend Otto Sørensen), 1916– ill. III. Title. PZ8.1.A8Man 1992   398.2—dc20   [E]   91-37599

The Man Who Kept House

by P. C. Asbjørnsen and J. E. Moe

illustrated by Svend Otto S.

Margaret K. McElderry Books • New York

Maxwell Macmillan Canada, Toronto • Maxwell Macmillan International, New York, Oxford, Singapore, Sydney

THERE ONCE was a man who was always cross because
he thought that his wife never did enough work in the
house. One evening, he came home tired from
harvesting, and began to grumble and to scold his wife.

"Dear husband, don't be so angry!" said his wife. "Tomorrow we can swap jobs. I'll go out with the harvesters and you can do the housework."

The man was quite satisfied with his wife's suggestion, and agreed to it. Early the next morning, the wife put the scythe over her shoulder and went out to the meadow to harvest, and the man stayed at home to do the housework.

He thought he would start by churning, because he
wanted to have butter for his dinner. But after churning
for a while, he grew thirsty and went down to the cellar
to draw some beer.

He took the stopper out of the beer barrel, but just as he was filling his mug with beer, he heard the pig come into the kitchen.

With the stopper still in his hand, he darted up the cellar steps to get to the pig before it managed to upset the butter churn.

He was too late. The pig had already knocked the churn over and was guzzling up the cream that had flowed all over the floor. The man flew into a terrible rage, forgot all about the barrel of beer, and began to chase the pig.

He caught up with it at the door and gave it such a
hard kick that it fell flat on its back and stayed there.

Suddenly, the man realized that he still had the stopper in his hand, but by the time he got back down to the cellar, the beer barrel was nearly empty.

He filled the churn again with milk and started churning once more, for he did want butter for his dinner.

After a while, he remembered that the cow was still in her stall and had not had a thing to eat or drink all morning.

There wasn't time now to take her to the field. He
would put her up on the roof instead. The roof was
made of sod and was covered with long juicy grass.

The man laid a plank against the roof and got the cow up onto it.

He didn't want to leave the butter churn alone again because the baby could easily knock it over. So he strapped the churn to his back.

Then he went out to get water for the cow.
He took the bucket to draw water from the well.

But when he bent over the edge of the well, the cream poured out of the butter churn and ran down his neck.

It would soon be dinnertime, and he still had no butter.

Well, he had better make some porridge for dinner and forget about the butter. So he hung a pot of water and oatmeal over the fire.

But the cow could fall off the roof and break her legs or her neck, so he climbed up to tether her.

He tied one end of the rope around the cow's neck and put the other end down the chimney.

Back in the kitchen, he tied the other end of the
rope around his leg. The water was nearly boiling, and
he had to start stirring the porridge.

While he was doing this, the cow fell off the roof
anyhow and pulled the man up the chimney by the leg.

The man was stuck, and, outside, the cow was
dangling in the air and could neither get up nor down.

Out in the field, the man's wife had been working hard all morning. Now it was time for her husband to call her in to dinner.

Time dragged on and nothing happened, so in the end she decided to go home anyhow.

When she saw the poor cow hanging by its neck, she climbed onto the roof and cut the rope with her scythe.

The man fell back down the chimney, and when his wife came into the kitchen, she found him standing on his head in the porridge pot.

Never again did the man complain about the way his wife kept house.